Bats at the Ballgame

BY BRIAN LIES

HOUGHTON MIFFLIN BOOKS FOR CHILDREN   HOUGHTON MIFFLIN HARCOURT   BOSTON   NEW YORK   2010

For my father-in-law, Sam Keith, who missed seeing his team take the Series— but never stopped believing.

And thanks to Steven Krasner, for deepening my understanding of baseball.

Houghton Mifflin Books for Children is an imprint of Houghton Mifflin Harcourt Publishing Company.

www.hmhbooks.com

The text of this book is set in 18-point Legacy.
The illustrations are acrylic paint on Strathmore paper.

Library of Congress Cataloging-in-Publication Data

Lies, Brian.
  Bats at the ballgame / written and illustrated by Brian Lies.
    p. cm.
  Summary: Two teams of bats play an exciting nighttime baseball game.
  ISBN 978-0-547-24970-4
  [1. Stories in rhyme. 2. Bats—Fiction. 3. Baseball—Fiction.] I. Title.
  PZ8.3.L618Bar 2010
  [E]—dc22

                    2009049694

Manufactured in Singapore
TWP 10 9 8 7 6 5 4 3 2 1
4500218527

Dusk creeps in, and day is done.
The last few rays of stubborn sun
cling to hilltop, tree, and town.
We wish that we could *push* it down!

Restless wings begin to itch—
excitement's at a fever pitch.
At last it's time, and with a sigh,
we hustle out to diamond sky.

Hurry up! Come one—come all!
We're off to watch the bats play ball!

How could any bat forget?
In all the countless years we've met,
it seems the team we'll play tonight
has beaten us in every fight.

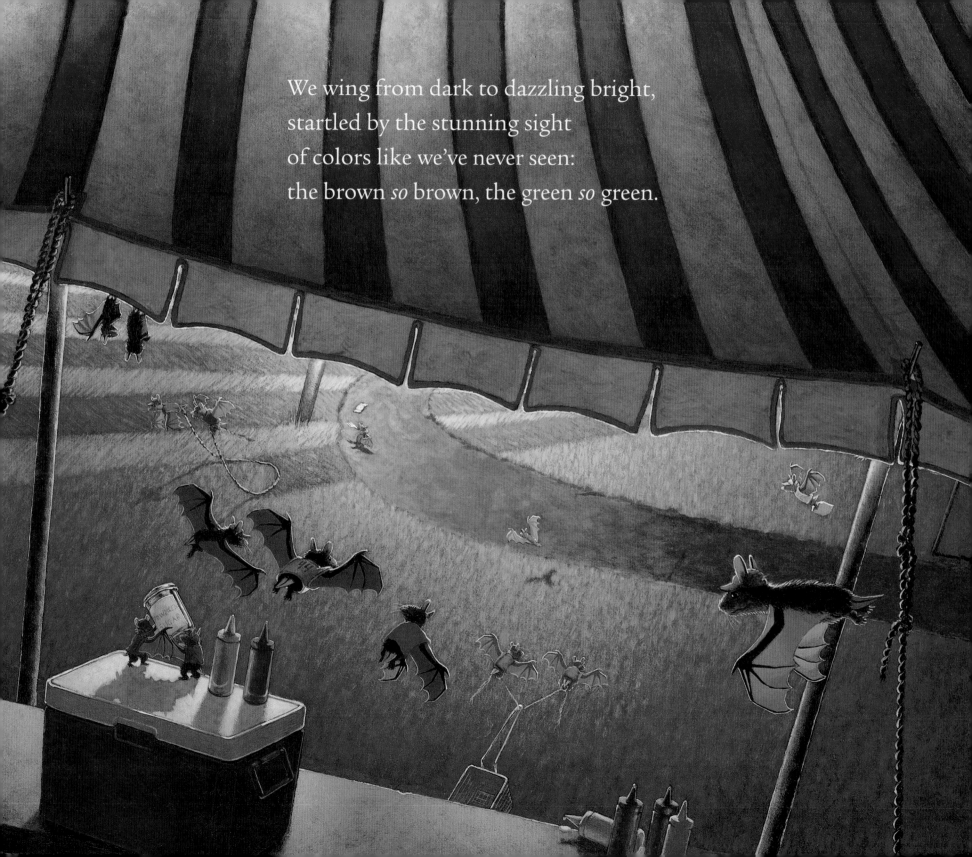

We wing from dark to dazzling bright,
startled by the stunning sight
of colors like we've never seen:
the brown *so* brown, the green *so* green.

A flying vendor flutters near.
"*Mothdogs! Get yer mothdogs here!*"
Raise a wing and catch a snack:
"*Perhaps you'd like some Cricket Jack?*"

We show our tickets, find our places,
watch the grounds crew lay the bases.

They roll the foul lines, rake the mound,
shape the field, and smooth the ground.

Sudden silence—then a cheer:
Hooray! The baseball bats are here!

A bat star sings our anthem song.
With wing on heart, we sing along,
and when she's done, the umpires call,
"Welcome, fans—and now . . . *play ball!*"

Something *changes* with those words.
We feel a magic shift,
and ride the currents of the game
as time is set adrift.

At first, we're full of reckless joy—
their batters strike out fast.
But when *our* batters strike out too,
our laughter doesn't last.

Our players muddle through the game
from innings two through five.
With nothing chalked up in the sixth,
they haven't come alive.

But in the seventh, signs of life!
. . . Too bad it's not *our* team.
Their fearless flyer cruises home
and tramples on our dream.

We find a golden moment
in the middle of it all:
The batter swings, it's going foul—
we reach . . . and catch the ball!

"Get it going! Throw a strike!"
We flap and howl and frown.
The seventh-inning stretch arrives

We shake our feet and raise our wings.
In voices high and strong,
together, all the fans belt out

Then back at bat, our batters swing,
but can't gain any ground.
There doesn't seem to be a way
to turn this game around!

Grandbats talk of better times,
of fields and heroes past.
Their thoughts slide homeward

through the years,

across eternal grass.

Then—*CRACK!*—the echo rockets 'round
and yanks us to today.
The bat at bat has smashed the ball,
its cover torn away.

Our flyer swoops from base to base,
and if he scores, we're tied!

And now the play is at the plate,
and now the bats collide.

So, was the flyer safe?

Or did the catcher have the ball?

When the dust has settled down,
the umpire makes the call:

"OUT!"

The crowd erupts and hollers,
"NO! You've lost your mind!
Can't you see that bat was safe?
Fire the ump! He's blind!"

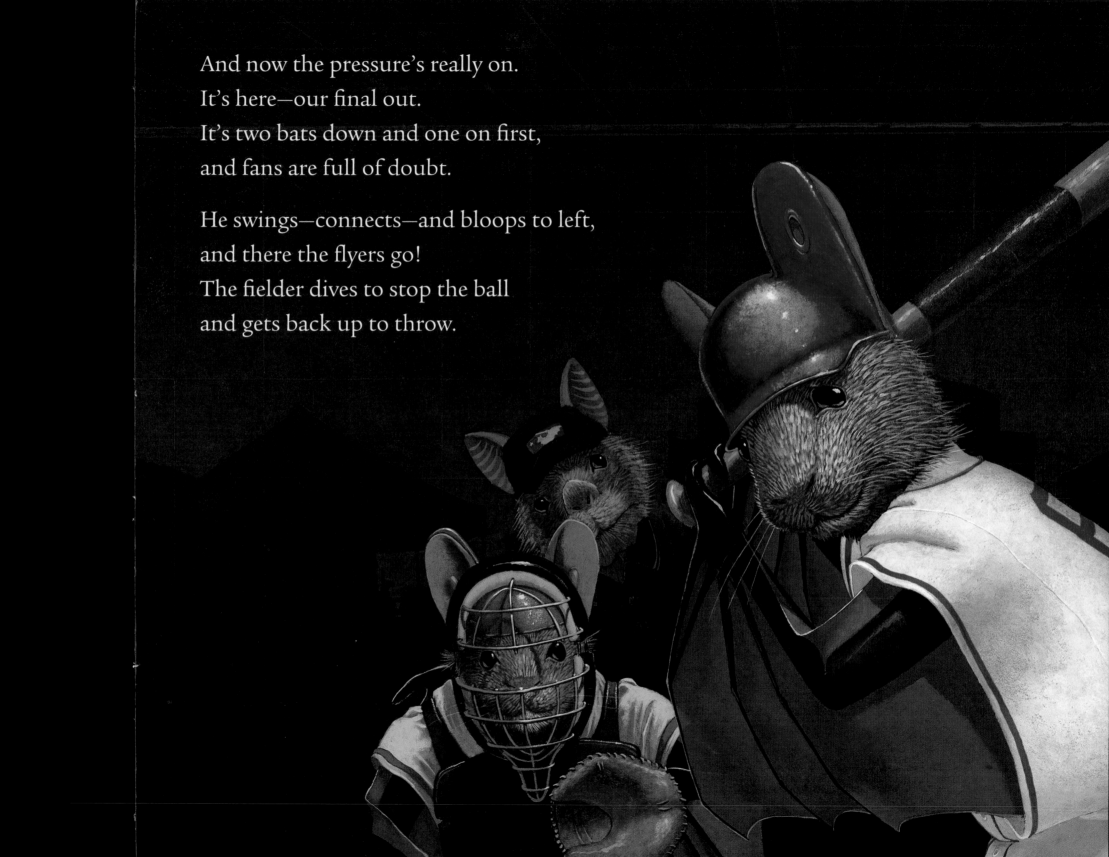

And now the pressure's really on.
It's here—our final out.
It's two bats down and one on first,
and fans are full of doubt.

He swings—connects—and bloops to left,
and there the flyers go!
The fielder dives to stop the ball
and gets back up to throw.

The play's to second. There it goes . . .

. . . *IT HITS THAT PESKY POLE!*

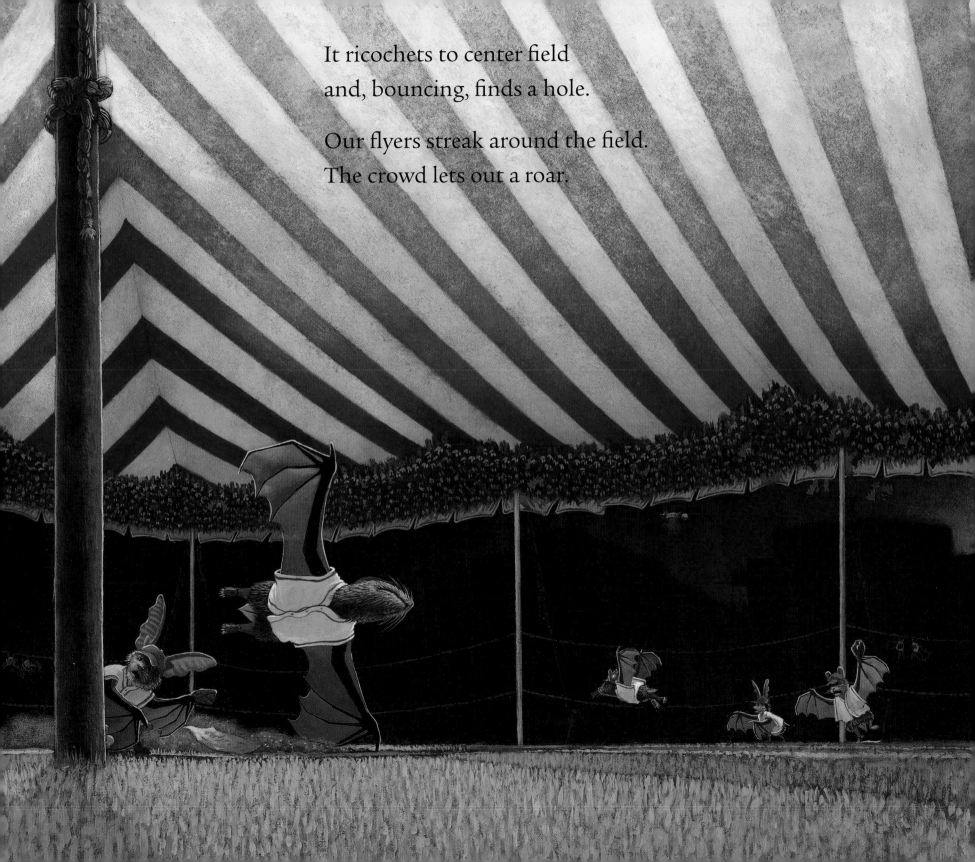

It ricochets to center field
and, bouncing, finds a hole.

Our flyers streak around the field.
The crowd lets out a roar.

The throw to home is not in time,
and both our flyers score!

That's it!
We won!
Can you *believe*?!
Now nothing can erase
the thrill that thunders in our hearts,
the grin on every face.

But in the east, the sky's aflame.
We feel ejected from the game!
Still astonished that we won,
we speed to beat the rising sun.

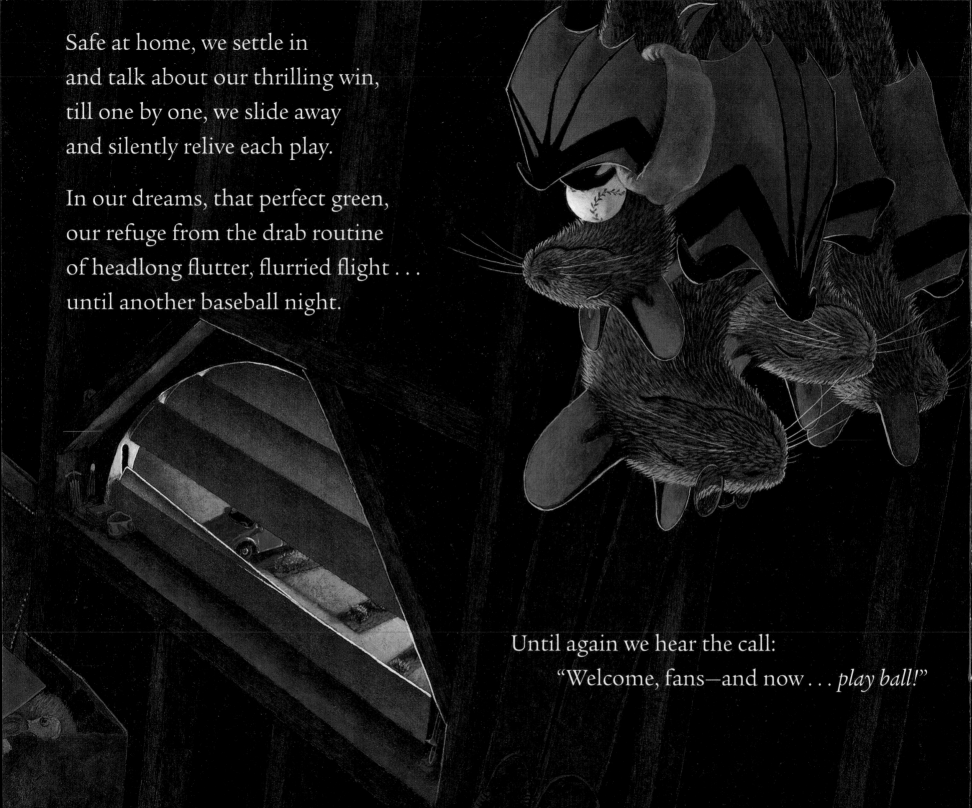

Safe at home, we settle in
and talk about our thrilling win,
till one by one, we slide away
and silently relive each play.

In our dreams, that perfect green,
our refuge from the drab routine
of headlong flutter, flurried flight . . .
until another baseball night.

Until again we hear the call:
"Welcome, fans—and now . . . *play ball!*"